HACHIKO

WAITS

LESLÉA NEWMAN

ILLUSTRATED BY
MACHIYO KODAIRA

HACHIKO

WAITS

SCHOLASTIC INC.
NEW YORK TORONTO LONDON AUCKLAND SYDNEY
MEXICO CITY NEW DELHI HONG KONG BUENOS AIRES

Note to Readers:
Words and phrases of Japanese origin
are listed in the glossary with pronunciation.
When a word is plural, an "s" has been added
to conform to the rules of English grammar.

ISBN-13: 978-0-545-07182-6
ISBN-10: 0-545-07182-8

Text copyright © 2004 by Lesléa Newman.
Illustrations copyright © 2004 by Machiyo Kodaira. All rights reserved.
Published by Scholastic Inc., 557 Broadway, New York, NY 10012, by arrangement with Henry Holt and Company, LLC. SCHOLASTIC and associated logos are trademarks and/or registered trademarks of Scholastic Inc. Lexile is a registered trademark of MetaMetrics, Inc.

12 11 10 9 8 7 6 5 4 3 2 1   8 9 10 11 12 13/0

Printed in the U.S.A.   23

First Scholastic printing, February 2008

CONTENTS

CONTENTS

When Professor Eizaburo Ueno woke up, he liked to play a game with his golden-brown puppy, Hachi. He lay on his *futon*, not moving a muscle. He did not even open his eyes. Could he fool Hachi into thinking he was asleep? Not a chance. Hachi knew the instant his master was awake and told him so by pushing his cold, wet nose into the Professor's hand.

"Good morning, Hachi." The Professor sat up and rubbed the soft patch of white fur that ran from the puppy's nose up between his eyes and stopped just below his pointy ears. "Did you sleep well, little friend?"

Hachi answered by wagging his fluffy, curled tail back and forth with great enthusiasm.

"I am glad you had such a fine night," the Professor said as he put on his glasses and rose from his silk sleeping mat. "Now come along, Hachi. Let us start the day." He motioned to the puppy, who followed along as the Professor washed himself, put on a dark blue *kimono* and headed downstairs to eat the breakfast his housekeeper had prepared for him before she left for the marketplace.

The Professor entered the *tatami* room, walked across the straw mats covering the floor, and sat down on a cushion in front of a low wooden table.

He poured himself a cup of hot green tea. As he lifted the steaming teacup, he looked up at a calendar hanging on the wall. The page it was turned to had a beautiful picture of a bright yellow sun rising over Japan.

"April 1, 1924," the Professor read out loud. "It is going to be a good day, little friend." The Professor said this every day. He was a man of habit.

Professor Ueno began to eat his breakfast of *miso* soup, dried fish and seaweed, rice, cooked eggs, and pickled radishes. His housekeeper had also set out breakfast for Hachi: a bowl of rice with *miso* soup poured over it. Hachi went over to his bowl, sniffed at it once, and walked away. He sat in the doorway and gazed at his master with a pleading look in his dark brown eyes. The Professor knew what Hachi wanted, but he shook his head.

"No, Hachi. You cannot have *yakitori* for breakfast," he said. *Yakitori* was the puppy's favorite meal. "I will buy some for your supper tonight on my way home from the train station, and you can practice pulling the chicken off the skewers the way I taught you. Now eat your food."

Hachi stayed where he was, and again the Professor knew what he wanted. Hachi played this game with him every morning. He was a dog of habit.

"All right, Hachi." Professor Ueno went over to the dog's bowl and knelt down beside it. "Mmm." The Professor smacked his lips as he pretended to pick a bit of food out of the bowl and taste it. "What delicious rice this is, Hachi. Come and try a bite. Here."

He scooped up a tiny bit of rice with his index finger and held it out to Hachi. The dog licked his finger and began to eat.

"Did you enjoy your breakfast this morning?" the Professor asked when Hachi was done. Hachi looked up at him with two grains of white rice stuck to his wet black nose.

The Professor laughed. "Let me wash your face, little friend. You cannot go around looking like that." He tenderly wiped the dog's muzzle with the corner of his napkin. "What a handsome dog you are." Hachi sat up tall and straight, basking in his master's praise.

The Professor finished his tea and rose from his cushion. "Now it is time for your lesson, Hachi. Come."

Professor Ueno walked to the front entryway with Hachi at his heels. The *genkan* had a mat spread out along one wall, with several pairs of the Professor's shoes lined up neatly upon it. The Professor stepped out of his house slippers and into a pair of *geta*, the wooden clogs he wore outside. Then together he and Hachi walked out of the house, across the front porch, and into the yard.

"Look, Hachi." The Professor pointed to a tree in the yard that was full of pink buds about to bloom. "Soon it will be time for our cherry-blossom party."

He took a few deep breaths, filling his lungs with fresh spring air, then turned to face his dog. "Let us begin," he said to the puppy. "Hachi. Sit." The Professor gave the command in a serious tone of voice, and Hachi immediately sat.

"Good dog," said the Professor. "Hachi. Down." Hachi lowered his body onto the ground, and again his master complimented him.

"What a good dog you are." The Professor knelt down and rubbed the fur around Hachi's neck and shoulders. "What a smart dog you are, Hachi. What a clever dog you are." Professor Ueno praised Hachi in a

high-pitched voice as though he were talking to a baby.

"We will try two more things." The Professor stood up and lowered his voice. "Hachi. Heel." Professor Ueno took a few steps around the garden, and Hachi followed him, keeping close to his left side.

"Good dog. Hachi. Sit."

Hachi did as he was told.

"Now, Hachi. Speak," said the Professor. Hachi stared at him silently, his head tilted to one side.

"Hachi. Speak." The Professor repeated the command, but Hachi remained silent.

"*Wan-wan, wan-wan.*" Professor Ueno demonstrated for him, yipping like a young puppy, but Hachi did not respond. The Professor changed his bark. "*Wan-wan, wan-wan,*" he repeated in the deep growling voice of a large angry dog. Hachi just looked at him.

"All right." The Professor shook his head. "It seems you have nothing to say today. And it is time for me to go teach my other students. Come inside."

Professor Ueno changed into a suit and tie and gathered his books and papers together. Then he walked down the hallway to the *genkan* and put on a pair of leather shoes. He left the house, and Hachi followed him to the front gate.

"Hachi. Sit," the Professor said. "What a good dog you are." He bent down until he was almost nose to nose with the puppy. "What a fine dog you are," he said softly. "Hachi, you are the best dog in all of Japan." He gave Hachi a few soft pats on the head, kissed the tip of his nose, and stood up.

"I will return at three o'clock. Farewell, little friend." The Professor turned from Hachi and pulled open the latch. As he went to shut the gate, one of his books dropped to the ground. When the Professor bent to pick it up, his glasses slipped down his nose and some papers flew out of his arms. The wind blew them down the street, and he raced after them without closing the gate properly. Hachi nosed it open and ran to be with his master.

"Hachi, how did you get out?" the Professor asked. "You must go home now." The Professor pointed toward the gate and spoke in a stern voice, but Hachi did not move. The Professor took a step back toward the house, but Hachi did not follow. He sat down right where he was and stared at the Professor.

Professor Ueno sighed and looked at his watch. "Hachi, I am going to miss my train," he said. Hachi wagged his tail. The Professor sighed again and shook his head. He never could stay mad at his puppy for long.

"All right, little friend," he said, giving in. "Come on. Heel."

Overjoyed, Hachi spun around in a circle and then fell into step beside his master.

C H A P T E R   T W O

Shibuya was filled with tiled-roof houses, bordered by a river, and surrounded by large fields. The Professor and Hachi rounded a corner and made their way down a residential street lined with tall *keyaki* trees, their branches covered with clusters of small yellow blossoms. As they walked along, the road grew wider and a tall Shinto shrine with red wooden gates and a green roof came into view. Many people nodded good morning to the Professor as he passed, and they admired Hachi, who pranced along beside his master, his pointed ears pitched forward, his curled tail held high.

16

As the Professor and Hachi neared the train station, the streets grew busier with people rushing along on foot and bicycle. Merchants in dark blue *happi* jackets scurried by, pulling large two-wheeled wooden carts stacked high with boxes.

"Hachi. Sit," the Professor said as they stopped at a corner and waited for a green trolley to pass. Then they crossed the street to the stairway leading up to the train station.

Hachi lifted his nose and sniffed the air around the food stalls near the steps to the station. Each stall was decorated with brightly colored paper lanterns, and each sold different things to eat: noodles, *tofu*, egg and fish boiled in broth, and *yakitori*.

"The vendors do not open until later in the day," the Professor told Hachi. "And you have already had your breakfast, little friend. Come." He hurried up the steps to the train station, and Hachi hurried beside him.

"Good morning, Professor Ueno."

The Professor turned around and saw the Station Master, dressed in a crisp black uniform, white gloves, and red-brimmed hat, bowing in respect.

"Good morning, Mr. Yoshikawa."

"What a fine-looking dog you have there," the Station Master said. Hachi sat down and puffed out his chest proudly, as though he understood Mr. Yoshikawa's compliment.

"I do not know what to do with him," said the

Professor, reaching down to rest his hand at the back of Hachi's head. "He followed me here, and I was afraid I would miss my train if I took him back home."

"I will watch him for you," Mr. Yoshikawa said with another bow. "I would be happy to do you the favor."

"I could not ask you to do such a thing," said the Professor.

"Ah, but you did not ask," the Station Master pointed out. "I offered. I will keep him in my office."

"It is too much trouble."

"It is no trouble at all," Mr. Yoshikawa insisted. "On the contrary, it would be an honor for me to do such a small thing for a man of your position."

The Professor nodded as he thought over the Station Master's offer. "*Arigato*, Mr. Yoshikawa," he said, bowing in thanks. "That is very kind of you. I will return at three o'clock."

"We will be waiting for you," said Mr. Yoshikawa, bowing as well. "What is your dog's name?"

"His name is Hachi."

"*Hachi*? Why did you name him 'Eight'?"

"Eight is my lucky number because the *kanji* for eight is shaped like a fan held upside down and it is wider at the bottom than at the top," the Professor explained, using his finger to draw the shape of the Japanese character in the air. "That means that the future is wide open. And Hachi is the eighth dog I have owned, so he is sure to be lucky. He is smarter than any other dog I have trained. Already I have taught him to sit, to lie down, to come, and to heel. The only thing I cannot teach him is to bark."

"Perhaps it is better that he does not speak," remarked the Station Master. "Some dogs cannot be taught to stop barking."

"That is true," said the Professor, "but *Akitas* do not misbehave like that. They do not bark unless they think something is wrong. But I would still like to teach him, just to hear the sound of his voice."

He looked down at his puppy, but Hachi remained silent. "Ah, well," Professor Ueno said. "I am sure Hachi will speak to me when he has something important to say. Thank you again for offering to watch him." The Professor bowed to the Station Master. "He will listen to you. He is usually"—he looked down at his puppy once more—"a very good dog."

The Professor showed the Ticket Taker his train pass and walked with Hachi and the Station Master onto a platform that bordered the train tracks and was sheltered by a red roof. The platform was crowded with commuters and shoppers. Many of the men wore business suits and leather shoes as the Professor did, but some of the men, and most of the women, wore *kimonos* with wooden *geta* clogs or straw *zori* sandals on their feet.

While the Station Master patrolled the platform,

Professor Ueno stood beside a woman in a green cotton *kimono* patterned with butterflies and fastened at her waist with an obi the color of pale jade. Her belongings were all tied up in a green cloth *furoshiki*. She balanced the tidy bundle on her right palm. With her other hand, she smoothed her small son's sailor suit. When at last the woman was satisfied with the boy's school uniform, she brushed some wisps of hair away from his forehead with her fingertips.

"Look, *Okaasan*." The boy broke from his mother's fussing and pointed. "A dog is waiting for the train." He held his hand out toward Hachi, but his mother pulled it back.

"Yasuo, be careful. He might bite."

"He will not hurt you." The Professor knelt down between the boy and Hachi. "He is very gentle."

"What is his name?" asked the boy.

"His name is Hachi," answered the Professor as he stood up. "And I am Eizaburo Ueno."

"I am Mrs. Takahashi," said Yasuo's mother, bowing her head. "And this is Yasuo, my son. Yasuo is very curious."

As if to prove his mother's point, Yasuo bowed and immediately posed another question. "What kind of dog is Hachi?" he asked the Professor.

"Yasuo," Mrs. Takahashi said, "do not be such a bother."

"It is no bother," said the Professor. "I am happy to answer your question. Hachi is a very special dog called an *Akita-ken*," he said proudly. And then, being a professor, he could not stop himself from giving Yasuo and his mother a short lesson about the breed. "*Akitas* are known for their intelligence, loyalty, and extreme devotion. Many years ago when *Akitas* were first bred in the northern mountains of Honshu, only members of the Imperial family were permitted to own them. The breed is more than three hundred years old."

"How old is Hachi?" Yasuo asked.

"Oh, he is just a puppy. He is only six months old."

"I am much older that that," Yasuo boasted. He opened his hand, spread his fingers wide, and counted. "*Ichi.*" He pulled his thumb into his palm. "*Ni.*" He folded down his index finger. "*San, shi, go.*" Yasuo bent in the rest of his fingers and held up his closed fist with pride. "I am five years old," he said, "almost six, and today is my first day of school."

"I am going to school too," said the Professor.

Yasuo looked at him in surprise. "I thought grown-ups went to work," he said.

"I work at a school," the Professor explained. "I am a teacher in the Agricultural Department of Tokyo Imperial University. When you are older, maybe you will be in my class."

"I would like that," said Yasuo.

At exactly nine o'clock, the train appeared around the bend of the tracks, squealed into the station on squeaky brakes, and came to a halt. As the commuters rushed onto the train, the station filled with the noise of dozens of pairs of wooden *geta* clogs clacking against the platform.

The Professor stood still while everyone else hurried past him onto the train. "Hachi. Sit," he said.

Hachi sat and Professor Ueno bent down and looked into his dark brown eyes.

"What a good dog you are," the Professor said once the station had quieted. "What a fine dog you are," he repeated softly. "Hachi, you are the best dog in all of Japan." He stroked Hachi's head, kissed the tip of his nose, and straightened up. "I will return at three o'clock."

The Professor stepped inside the train just before it pulled away and waved to Hachi. "Farewell, little friend."

Hachi stayed right where he was on the platform, craning his neck to watch the departing train that held his master. When he could no longer see it, he sat a few minutes more, staring at the empty tracks.

Mr. Yoshikawa came up behind him and scratched his ears. "You are going to spend the day with me, Hachi," he said. "Come." Mr. Yoshikawa took a few steps back toward his office. But Hachi remained where he was, staring off in the direction the Professor's train had gone. Then he stood up, turned, and trotted toward the exit of the station.

"Hachi," Mr. Yoshikawa called, clapping his white gloves sharply. "Come back." Hachi ignored him and continued on his way.

"Hachi!" the Station Master cried. He hurried after the dog, but when Hachi saw he was being chased, he dashed through the station, down the steps, and out onto the street. Mr. Yoshikawa followed the dog down the stairs and tried to catch him, but he could not leave his post at the train station. In dismay he watched as the tip of Hachi's tail disappeared around a corner. What was he going to tell the Professor when he returned on the three o'clock train?

CHAPTER THREE

Professor Ueno packed up his books and left his class-
room in a hurry. He was so distracted by thoughts of
Hachi, he almost collided with a delivery boy on a bicycle, who was balancing a round tray stacked high with
lunch boxes and rice bowls above his shoulder. "Excuse
me." The Professor lowered his head in apology as the
delivery boy swerved out of his way.

Hoping Hachi had not caused the Station Master
any trouble, the Professor hurried along to board the
train that would take him from the university back to
Shibuya Station.

Mr. Yoshikawa looked up at the big round clock hanging from the ceiling in the center of the train station. It was almost three o'clock. Soon Professor Ueno would arrive, and the Station Master would have to tell him what had happened. The Professor had trusted him to take care of his dog, and he had not done his job.

All day long he had asked people waiting for their trains if they had seen Hachi. "He is a young golden-brown *Akita-ken* with a white patch of fur on his face," the Station Master said over and over.

Every hour or so Mr. Yoshikawa went down to ask the food vendors if they had noticed Hachi sniffing around their booths in search of a snack. He bought a bowl of *udon* from a vendor, quickly gobbled down the wide noodles, and then spent the better part of his noontime break searching the neighborhood for Hachi. But he had not been able to find him.

At five minutes before three o'clock, Mr. Yoshikawa walked out onto the platform and pulled at the tip of his red-brimmed hat. He looked to his right, the direction from which the train would arrive. There was no sign of it yet. Mr. Yoshikawa turned and looked to his left. He blinked once, then shook his head and blinked again, because he could not believe what he saw: a golden-brown *Akita-ken*!

The Station Master rushed over to the dog. "Hachi?" he asked. The dog thumped his tail once at the sound of his name. "Where have you been?" Mr. Yoshikawa asked, rubbing the dog's neck and shoulders. "I have been worried about you."

Hachi stared into his eyes, mute.

"Well, never mind," Mr. Yoshikawa said, giving Hachi a pat on the head. "I am very happy that you are here." And just as the words left his mouth, the train entered the station and ground to a halt. Professor Ueno was the first one to step off.

"Hello, little friend!" he called, his voice full of happiness. Hachi ran to his master, licked each of his fingers, and then spun in circles before him.

Yasuo and his mother followed the Professor off the train. "Look, *Okaasan*," Yasuo laughed. "The Professor's dog is making himself dizzy."

"He is dizzy with joy," said Mrs. Takahashi with a smile.

When Hachi stopped spinning, Yasuo called, "Here, Hachi," and held out his hand. The dog looked at the boy and wagged his tail, but he stayed at the side of his master.

"Thank you so much for watching him," the Professor said to the Station Master. "It was very kind of you to do me the favor."

"You are very welcome," said Mr. Yoshikawa.

"Was Hachi any trouble?" Professor Ueno asked.

Mr. Yoshikawa looked at the dog and lifted his eye-

brows. Hachi looked back at him with his mouth slightly open and his pink tongue hanging out, almost as though he were laughing.

"I do not know if he was trouble," the Station Master said. "Hachi left the station a few minutes after your train pulled away from the platform. I tried to catch him, but he ran too fast. I asked many people, and searched for him during my lunch hour, but I could not find him. And then out of nowhere" — Mr. Yoshikawa gestured toward the train station's entrance — "he returned just before three o'clock. It is as though he knew when you would arrive."

The Professor looked down at Hachi and beamed. Dogs could not tell time. Or could they? "That is most interesting," he said to the Station Master. "I am sorry he caused you so much trouble."

"There is no need to apologize," said Mr. Yoshikawa, "because the story has a happy ending."

"I thank you again," said the Professor, bowing his head. Then he turned to Hachi. "I always knew you were smart," he said. "Now I know you are even smarter than I thought. Little friend, you are the smartest dog in all of Japan."

From that day on, Hachi walked to the train station with Professor Ueno every morning and met his train every afternoon. The Professor knew that Hachi ran home after his train left the station because his house-keeper told him so. Hachi kept himself very busy while the Professor was at work. He cleaned his paws and chased his tail. He sniffed the wind and chewed on sticks. He often took long naps in the sun under the cherry tree in the yard. But he always woke up in time to return to the station to meet his master's train.

The Station Master checked the time as soon as

Hachi arrived. "Five minutes to three," he would announce, looking at the big clock hanging from the station's ceiling. "Hachi, you are always right on time. I could set that clock by you."

A year passed, and the Professor's routine did not change. He and Hachi walked to the train station in the spring, when the cherry blossoms bloomed, and in the summer, when the rains came. They walked to the train station in the autumn, when the leaves changed color, and in the winter, when the snow fell. The Professor was always the last one to step onto the train before it left in the morning, and he was always the first one to step off the train after it arrived in the afternoon. And Hachi was always there to meet him. He was never a minute early and never a minute late. And as soon as he saw the Professor, he always ran to his master, licked his fingers, and spun in joyful circles before him.

One morning in early May as the Professor and Hachi were taking their morning walk to the train station, Professor Ueno stopped to admire the many-colored fish-shaped banners hanging from bamboo poles outside the houses they passed. "Hachi. Sit. Look, little friend," the Professor said, pointing. "Those flags look like a type of fish called carp, and they have been hung in honor of *Tango-no-Sekku*, a special holiday that celebrates all the boys of Japan."

Hachi's eyes followed his master's finger toward the waving banners.

"It is traditional to hang a special carp flag for each boy in the family," the Professor told Hachi. "When I was young, a big red-and-white carp flag that looked exactly like that one flew for me." He gestured toward an especially large banner rippling in the wind.

"The carp is very strong and very brave, little friend. He must swim upstream against the current, and that takes great determination and perseverance. But once he does so, he knows he can overcome all of life's obstacles and difficulties. Every boy, including you, Hachi, must strive to be as strong and brave as the carp."

Hachi sat completely still with his ears thrust forward, listening carefully to the Professor as he always did when receiving such lessons from his master.

"Come, Hachi. It is time to catch my train. Heel." The Professor started off again, and Hachi fell into step beside him. It was a mild spring day, yet by the time Professor Ueno and Hachi walked up the steps to the train station, the Professor's face was covered with sweat. He removed his glasses and wiped his forehead with a clean white handkerchief.

"Good morning, Professor." The Station Master greeted Professor Ueno with a bow. "Hello, Hachi."

"Good morning, Mr. Yoshikawa." The Professor lifted his handkerchief and wiped his brow again.

"Are you not feeling well?" the Station Master asked, his voice full of concern. "Would you like a glass of water?"

"No, thank you. That is very kind of you, but I am fine," the Professor said, putting his handkerchief into his pocket. He showed the Ticket Taker his pass and walked through the doorway.

"Hachi!" Yasuo called. The Professor and Hachi crossed over to the platform.

"Happy Boys' Day, Yasuo," said the Professor.

"Thank you," said Yasuo. He ran his hands up and down the fur around Hachi's neck. "He has gotten so big."

"He stands almost two feet high now and weighs one hundred pounds. That is a good size for a male *Akita*," said the Professor, who never let an opportunity to teach go by.

"Feel his coat here." He guided Yasuo's hands to Hachi's chest. "This fur is his undercoat. It is thicker and softer than the rest of his fur. Once the undercoat has come in, the *Akita-ken* is full grown."

"I am still growing," said Yasuo. "I am going to be very tall."

"Taller than I am?" teased the Professor, who was not tall at all.

"I hope so," said Yasuo, standing up on his toes.

"Yasuo!" said his mother in a scolding voice. "The Professor is a man of respect. Do not be rude to him."

But Professor Ueno only laughed. "I am sure you will rise to great heights," he said to the boy.

The nine o'clock train arrived right on schedule. As

everyone clambered onto it, Professor Ueno leaned down to say good-bye to Hachi.

"What a good dog you are." He repeated the same words every day. "What a fine dog you are. Hachi, you are the best dog in all of Japan." He patted Hachi's head and kissed the tip of his nose.

"I will return at three o'clock," he reminded Hachi. "Farewell, little friend." The train pulled away, and the Professor waved as he always did.

Hachi stayed right where he was, watching the train as usual. But then he did something he had never done before. As the train picked up speed, Hachi chased after it and let out a loud bark.

"Wan-wan!" he called to Professor Ueno. And then again, *"Wan-wan! Wan-wan!"*

The Professor leaned out of the train with a worried look on his face. Was Hachi all right? But when he saw the dog standing on the platform and wagging his tail, he grinned and waved.

"Hachi, what a splendid voice you have," he called out proudly. "What a good dog you are. Farewell, little friend."

The Station Master walked over to Hachi and squatted down before him.

"What did you have to say to the Professor today that was so important?" he asked the *Akita-ken.*

But Hachi would not repeat himself. He merely turned and left for home.

At three o'clock that afternoon when the train pulled into Shibuya Station, Hachi sat in his usual spot by the tracks, his eyes focused on the first car's door. It slid open, and a woman in a blue-and-white *kimono* with a tiny baby strapped to her back stepped out. A man carrying a newspaper followed. Two young girls in matching blue skirts and white blouses with red kerchiefs tied around their necks came next. Where was the Professor? Hachi sat still as a statue, waiting. Finally Yasuo and his mother stepped onto the platform.

"Hachi!" Yasuo called. The dog barely looked at him. "*Okaasan*, where is the Professor? He was not on the train."

"Perhaps he was in another car," Mrs. Takahashi said, her eyes searching the platform. "I do not see him," she said. "Hachi, your master must have missed his train. Do not worry. I am sure he will be on the next one."

"Do not worry, Hachi," Yasuo repeated, patting the dog on the head.

Hachi sat up very tall and straight with his ears held erect, staring at the train tracks. When the next train arrived, he looked at each person who stepped out, but none of them was the Professor. Other trains came and went, each one discharging many passengers. Some people hurried by Hachi; others stopped and ran their hands along the dog's soft fur. Hachi paid no attention to any of them.

Hachi waited all afternoon and all evening as train after train pulled in and out of the station. Mr. Yoshikawa brought him water and tried to share a bowl of rice with him, but Hachi would not eat. Finally it was midnight, and the last train arrived at the station. Professor Ueno was not on it.

"Where can the Professor be?" the Station Master wondered out loud. He took off his hat and scratched the side of his head. "This is not like him. He never misses his train."

The Station Master put his hat back on and pulled the brim down low over his eyes. "I am sorry, Hachi. I have to close the station now. And you must go home. Go." Mr. Yoshikawa pointed his white glove at the stairway.

Hachi's eyes followed the Station Master's finger, but the rest of him did not move.

"I am sorry, Hachi, but you must go." Mr. Yoshikawa was kind yet firm as he forced Hachi through the station toward the exit.

Hachi did not want to leave, but he had no choice. The station was locked up tight behind him.

CHAPTER FIVE

The next morning, Yasuo and his mother arrived at the train station a little before nine o'clock. The day was unusually warm and humid; it felt more like July than May. The air on the platform was heavy and still, and Mrs. Takahashi untucked a white silk fan decorated with pink flowers from her *obi* and waved it lightly in front of her face.

"Where are the Professor and Hachi?" Yasuo asked his mother.

"I do not know," she said, searching the platform. Mrs. Takahashi's eyes swept over a sea of colorful

39

kimonos in search of the Professor's dark brown business suit. "Maybe the Professor is away. Or maybe he is ill." Mrs. Takahashi looked around once more. "I am sure he will be here tomorrow. Come, Yasuo. Here is the train."

That afternoon, Professor Ueno was not on the train that Yasuo and his mother rode back to Shibuya Station. And he was not on the platform when they stepped off the train. But Hachi was there, sitting in his usual spot, alert and waiting.

"This is most unusual. Now I am worried," said Yasuo's mother. "Let us wait for the next train."

Mrs. Takahashi and Yasuo walked over to a wooden bench and sat down. It wasn't long before the next train pulled into the station and discharged its passengers. Yasuo and Mrs. Takahashi watched as a crowd of people hurried by: a woman carrying a *furoshiki* and leading a small child by the hand; high-school boys in their navy-blue school uniforms with gold buttons marching up the front of their jackets; and young girls with full serge skirts tied over their bright *kimonos*.

Hachi sat where he was, sniffing the air, his eyes scanning the faces of the many people around him. Yasuo and his mother searched the crowd as well, but they did not see the Professor. They sat on the bench while two more trains pulled into the station. Many people departed from the trains and hurried past Hachi to get out of the station. But Professor Ueno was not one of them.

"Come, Yasuo." Mrs. Takahashi stood up. "Let us speak to the Station Master. Perhaps he knows something."

Yasuo's mother bowed to Mr. Yoshikawa. "We are curious about Professor Ueno," she said. "He was not on the train today."

"A terrible thing has happened." Mr. Yoshikawa removed his hat and spoke in a hushed voice. "Professor Ueno took ill while he was at the university yesterday. His heart stopped beating. Another professor who works with him came to my office and told me."

Yasuo's mother knelt down and took her son's hand. "Yasuo, the Professor has died," she said in a small, gentle voice.

"But why?" Yasuo asked. "He was not old."

"No one knows why it happened," said the Station Master.

"We will never see the Professor again," Yasuo whispered. As he stood quietly beside his mother, his chin trembled and his eyes grew moist. He would miss seeing Professor Ueno every day. And what would become of Hachi? Yasuo turned to the dog waiting patiently on the platform amid a steady stream of commuters. Tears spilled down Yasuo's cheeks.

"But what about . . ." Yasuo's words caught in his throat.

"I do not know what to do," said Mr. Yoshikawa, looking at the dog. "Hachi arrived just before three o'clock as he always does. He does not know his master will never return."

An idea took shape in Yasuo's mind. "*Okaasan*," he said, looking up at his mother. "May we take Hachi home with us? Please?"

"I am sure he will not be any trouble," the Station Master said. "He is very smart and well behaved. I have never heard him growl. And until yesterday, I had never heard him bark."

"I must think about it," said Mrs. Takahashi.

She looked over at Hachi as he sat perfectly still among the mass of people swirling around him, and just at that moment, he glanced over his shoulder and looked at her. Then his somber gaze returned to the train tracks.

"Please, *Okaasan*," Yasuo said. "I will take good care of him. I promise."

Yasuo held his breath as his mother thought. "I will do it for the Professor," she said at last. "He was a very kind man."

"*Arigato, Okaasan*," Yasuo said with a bow. Then he went over to the doorway. "Here, Hachi!" he called, slapping his thighs. But the dog did not move.

Yasuo ran out onto the platform. "You are coming home with *Okaasan* and me," he told the *Akita-ken*.

Hachi stared up at Yasuo, but at the sound of an approaching train, he fixed his eyes upon the tracks.

Yasuo stepped up right beside him and then began walking away. "Hachi. Heel." Yasuo spoke in the stern voice he had heard the Professor use when giving the dog a command. "Hachi. Heel," he said again. But Hachi would not obey him.

"I will get you something to lead him with," said Mr. Yoshikawa.

He disappeared into his office for a minute and then returned with a long piece of rope. He tied one end around Hachi's neck and handed the other end to Yasuo.

"Come, Hachi," Yasuo said. "We are going home." He pulled at the rope, but Hachi would not budge. "He is stronger than I am. *Okaasan*, you must help me."

Yasuo and his mother tugged on the rope. Hachi stood his ground. The Station Master gave them a hand, and at last, with great reluctance, Hachi began to move.

"He is not happy," Yasuo said as they led Hachi out of the station and down the steps.

"He will get used to us," Yasuo's mother said as they half-pulled, half-dragged Hachi away.

CHAPTER SIX

When Yasuo and his mother got home, they took off their shoes and brought Hachi inside. Yasuo put a bowl of fresh water down on the floor of the front entryway for him.

"What will he eat?" Yasuo asked his mother.

"He will eat what we eat," she answered. "Rice and fish and vegetables. We do not have money to buy special food for him."

"Come inside, Hachi," Yasuo called, but the dog was not interested in leaving the *genkan* to explore the rest of Yasuo's house. He sat in front of the door and stared at it.

"He does not like it here," Yasuo said sadly.

"He needs time to get used to his new life," said Mrs. Takahashi.

Yasuo knelt down next to Hachi and stroked the fur on his back. He spoke to him in a calm, soothing voice.

"I know you miss the Professor," he said. At the word *professor*, Hachi's ears swiveled back. "I miss him too. But you will like living with us, Hachi. I will give you bits of fish and meat and other good things to eat, and I will play with you. We will have fun together." Yasuo offered his hand to Hachi, hoping he would lick it. But the dog just stayed where he was, staring at the door.

"Poor Hachi," Yasuo said. "You are hoping that the door will open and the Professor will walk through it. I would like that to happen too. But it is not possible." Yasuo shook his head sadly. If only he knew a way to make the *Akita-ken* understand his words. Yasuo spoke to the dog a little while longer, then fell silent and sat quietly beside him, hoping his presence would bring the dog comfort.

"Yasuo," Mrs. Takahashi called to her son, "it is time to start your homework."

Yasuo brought his schoolbooks into the front entryway to be near Hachi. He opened a book and began to practice his reading. A short time later he heard footsteps outside the front door. It was his father coming home from work.

"*Otoosan*, please do not come in yet," Yasuo called through the door. "We have a surprise for you." Then he called to his mother. "*Okaasan*, please come help me with Hachi."

Yasuo's mother came to the *genkan*, and together she and Yasuo held on to Hachi so that he would not run away.

"You may come in now, *Otoosan*," Yasuo said. "But please slide the door open quickly, and then slide it shut tight behind you."

"Hello, who is this?" Yasuo's father asked upon seeing the big golden-brown dog.

"This is Hachi," Yasuo said. "He is Professor Ueno's dog."

"And where is the Professor?" asked Mr. Takahashi as he stepped out of his work shoes and into his cloth house slippers.

Mrs. Takahashi motioned to her husband to follow her into the next room. A few minutes later, Yasuo's father came back to speak to his son.

"I hear that Hachi is going to live with us," he said to Yasuo. "You know that taking care of a dog is a big responsibility."

"Yes, *Otoosan*."

"Do you feel that you are ready to take on such a big responsibility?"

"Yes, *Otoosan*," Yasuo said again.

"He is a young dog," Mr. Takahashi said, indicating

the back of Hachi's head. "He will live for many years, Yasuo. It will be your duty to take care of him for a long time. Even on the days that you would prefer to do something else."

"I understand, *Otoosan*."

Mr. Takahashi squatted down and patted the dog on the head. "Hello, Hachi," he said softly. Then he turned to Yasuo. "He is very beautiful."

"He is an *Akita-ken*," Yasuo said.

"I have heard of the *Akita*," said Yasuo's father. "They are very brave and very smart. We will take him for a walk after we eat. Now go inside and change out of your uniform, Yasuo. I will put on a *kimono* and then we will have supper."

When the evening meal was ready, Yasuo and his father went into the *tatami* room. They sat down on cushions in front of a low dining table next to a small alcove. In the alcove was a tall black lacquer vase holding a pair of purple irises that Yasuo's mother had taken great care to arrange in a pleasing manner.

Mrs. Takahashi brought in three bowls of clear soup, three bowls of rice, and three plates of *tempura*, and then sat down with her family to eat.

Yasuo used his chopsticks to pick out the pieces of *tofu* and vegetables floating in his soup and then lifted the lacquer bowl up to his lips and drank the hot, clear broth. Next he turned to the *tempura*. The pieces of

batter-dipped, fried shrimp and vegetables were balanced in a perfect circle on Yasuo's plate. He ate a few
pieces along with some rice and then tried to coax
Hachi away from the door with what remained on his
dish.

"Here, Hachi," Yasuo said, offering the dog a few
bits of shrimp. "Try some of this." But Hachi did not
even turn his head to sniff at the food. He would not
even take a sip of water. He just stayed where he was in
front of the door with his back to Yasuo's family.

"May we take Hachi for a walk now?" Yasuo asked
as soon as his father put down his chopsticks.

"Maybe that will make him feel better." Mr.
Takahashi took a last sip of tea and rose from his cushion. "We will feed him when we return. Come."

Yasuo's father put one end of the rope around
Hachi's neck and held the other end tightly as he slid
open the door. But he was not prepared for Hachi's
great strength. As soon as the door was open, Hachi
burst out of the house, yanking the end of the rope right
out of Mr. Takahashi's hand.

"Hachi, come back!" Yasuo cried, but the dog raced
away. Yasuo and his father dashed up the street, but
they were no match for Hachi, who ran faster than the
wind.

Mr. Takahashi turned to his son. "I am sorry,
Yasuo."

"It is not your fault, *Otoosan*. Hachi did not want to live with us. We are not his family."

Yasuo's father put his arm around his son's shoulders. "*Akitas* are very intelligent. They were bred to be hunting dogs. I have heard that an *Akita-ken* can even bring down a bear. Do not worry, Yasuo. Hachi will take care of himself."

"But what is there to hunt in Shibuya?" Yasuo asked. And his father did not have an answer.

CHAPTER SEVEN

The morning after Hachi disappeared, Yasuo woke up early. He washed himself quickly, put on his school uniform, and hurried into the *tatami* room to speak to his mother.

"Good morning, *Okaasan*," Yasuo said. "Did Hachi come back?"

"No," Mrs. Takahashi said. "*Otoosan* looked for him before he left for work, but he did not find him. I am sorry, Yasuo. Come sit down and eat something."

Yasuo sat on his cushion, picked up his chopsticks,

and tried to eat some rice, but he could not. He could not even take a sip of *miso* soup. There was no room for food in his stomach. It was too full of sadness.

"We will never see the Professor again," Yasuo said, his voice heavy with sorrow. "And now we will never see Hachi again."

Yasuo stood up from his cushion and gathered his schoolbooks, moving slow as a turtle. As soon as he and his mother left the house, he began to search for the Professor's dog.

"Hachi! Hachi!" Yasuo called, cupping his hands around his mouth. Then he stood very still and listened, but he did not hear the footsteps of the *Akita-ken*. Yasuo took two more steps, stopped, and cupped his hands again. "Hachi!"

Yasuo did this all the way to the train station, but it was no use. Hachi was nowhere to be found.

The Station Master greeted them eagerly at the top of the stairs. "Good morning, Mrs. Takahashi. Good morning, Yasuo," he said. "How is Hachi?"

"He ran away," said Yasuo, looking down at his shoes. "We do not know where he is."

"He is such a handsome dog. I am sure someone will take him in and care for him," said Mr. Yoshikawa, trying to make Yasuo feel better.

"I hope so," said Mrs. Takahashi.

Yasuo had a hard time paying attention to his

schoolwork that day, and he did not do well, even in math, his favorite subject. Usually Yasuo moved the beads of his abacus swiftly along their rods and called out the answers to addition problems long before his classmates did. But today he could not concentrate.

All morning long Yasuo worried about Hachi. Was he hungry? Was he thirsty? Was he safe? He knew it was not his father's fault, but still, he wished that somehow *Otoosan* could have held on to Hachi's rope more tightly. But Yasuo knew Hachi would have run away eventually. The *Akita* would never rest until he found the Professor. And as soon as Yasuo had that thought, an idea crossed his mind. Maybe, just maybe . . .

Yasuo's mother met him when school let out, and they walked to the station. When they boarded the train to Shibuya, Yasuo pulled his mother through the train until they stood in the first car right in front of the door.

"Why are you in such a hurry today?" Yasuo's mother asked.

Yasuo did not answer. He wanted to keep his thoughts to himself, hoping if he did so, what he yearned for would be true.

As soon as the train pulled into Shibuya Station and the door slid open, Yasuo leapt onto the platform. And just as he had hoped, there was the golden-brown *Akita-ken,* sitting in his usual spot, waiting for the Professor.

"Hachi!" Yasuo cried, throwing his arms around the dog's neck.

Hachi wagged his tail once and allowed Yasuo to hug him, but he did not stray from his task of looking up at each passenger who stepped off the train, hoping to catch sight of his master's face.

Mr. Yoshikawa hurried up to Yasuo and his mother. "I am so glad you are here to see for yourself that Hachi is all right. He arrived a little before three o'clock, just like always."

"I knew he would be here," said Yasuo. He stroked Hachi's neck.

"He has not given up hope," said Mrs. Takahashi. She watched as the dog's dark eyes searched the face of every single person on the platform. "He is very devoted."

"Would you like to help me take care of him?" the Station Master asked Yasuo. "He will need food and water every day. He will need his thick coat brushed to keep it shiny and clean." The Station Master looked over at Hachi. "And he will need someone to keep him company."

"I will come every day after school." Yasuo looked up at his mother. "Please, *Okaasan*."

Mrs. Takahashi knelt down beside her son. "Yasuo, do you remember what *Otoosan* said about taking care of a dog?"

"Yes, *Okaasan*. He said it was a big responsibility and it would be my duty for a very long time."

"Do you feel that you are ready to take on such a big responsibility?"

"Yes, *Okaasan*."

Yasuo's mother looked at her son. She looked at the Station Master. She looked at Hachi. Another train screeched into the station, discharged a horde of passengers, and left the platform. Mrs. Takahashi watched Hachi's head move to the left and to the right, as he made sure to look at the face of every person who came his way.

"Yes," she said at last. "It is what the Professor would have wanted. I know you will be good to Hachi. And he will come back to the train station every day because he knows you will care for him."

"No, *Okaasan*," said Yasuo. "He will come back to the train station every day to wait for the Professor."

CHAPTER EIGHT

And so it went, day after day after day. Hachi waited at the train station in the spring, when the cherry blossoms bloomed, and in the summer, when the rains came. He waited in the autumn, when the leaves changed color, and in the winter, when the snow fell. Day after day after day Hachi arrived at the train station just before three o'clock to meet the Professor. Day after day after day he was disappointed. But he never gave up hope.

Mr. Yoshikawa did not know where Hachi went when he locked up the station at midnight. He did not know where Hachi slept. He did not know where Hachi spent the morning and the early part of the afternoon. But he did know where Hachi would be every day just before three o'clock: sitting on the platform waiting for his master. But instead of the Professor, now it was Yasuo who stepped off the train.

Yasuo had turned ten on his last birthday, and now he was old enough to travel back and forth to school by himself. "Hello, Hachi," Yasuo called to the dog sitting on the platform.

Hachi looked at Yasuo for a brief second, thumped his tail against the ground twice, and then turned his attention back to the crowd of people getting off the train.

"I will be there in a minute with your food," Yasuo said, going into the Station Master's office to fill Hachi's bowl. He placed it in front of the dog and stroked the fur between his ears while he ate.

A small woman with thin gray hair pulled back in a bun came to stand next to Yasuo. "Is this the dog I have heard about who waits for his master?" she asked.

"Yes, this is Hachi," Yasuo answered.

The woman studied him for a few minutes. "May I pet him?" she asked.

"Yes. He will not hurt you. He is very gentle." Yasuo said the same words to the woman the Professor had said to him on the day they had met, years before.

"I am sorry for your sadness, Hachi," the woman said as she stroked his neck.

Hachi turned to her for a moment, and his ears slid back at the softness of her voice. She gently rubbed the white patch of fur between Hachi's eyes as he looked at her. Then a train approached the platform, and Hachi returned his gaze to the railroad tracks.

As the train discharged its passengers, Hachi sat up straight and turned his head to the right, to the left, and to the right again, looking at all the people who passed him. A man who wore a pair of black-framed glasses and a business suit, and was about Professor Ueno's height, walked toward Hachi. The dog sat up even taller and began to tremble all over, his nose sniffing the air. But the man hurried past, and Hachi, realizing that the man was a stranger, stilled himself and continued his search for the Professor.

"That man looked like Hachi's master," Yasuo explained to the old woman who was watching the dog intently.

The woman reached out to stroke Hachi's fur again. "Hachi, you are a very good dog," she said to him. "And your master was a very good man."

Yasuo picked up Hachi's bowl and looked at the woman. "Did you know Professor Ueno?" he asked.

"No," the woman answered. "But it is clear to me that he was a fine man. That is why Hachi continues to hope and to wait. He remembers the kindness of his master."

One day a man in a dark gray suit and hat whom Yasuo had never seen before came to the train station. He stood next to Hachi, watching him as several trains arrived, discharged their passengers, and departed. The man studied the way Hachi sat, looking up at each and every face that passed him, and how his own face was filled with longing. He took photographs of Hachi with an expensive-looking camera. Then the man asked Yasuo many questions about the dog and wrote everything down in a little notebook.

The next day when Yasuo arrived at the train station, Mr. Yoshikawa handed him a newspaper. "Look, here is a picture of our Hachi," he said, pointing to a page.

" 'Hachiko Waits,' " Yasuo read the headline out loud. Then he read the caption underneath Hachi's photo: " '*Chuken* Hachiko sits at Shibuya Station waiting for his master.' "

"I think he has earned the official name of 'Hachiko,' " said the Station Master. "After all, he is our beloved Hachi, and he deserves a name of respect."

"I will tell him," Yasuo said as he crossed the platform. "Look, here is your photo, Hachiko." Yasuo emphasized the term of honor and affection the newspaper had added to the end of Hachi's name.

Hachi wagged his tail at the sound of Yasuo's voice and turned to smell the newspaper he held, but found it of little interest. As always, his main concern was the people on the platform who had just come off a train.

"And here is your new name." Yasuo held the paper out again. "*Chuken* Hachiko, the faithful dog Hachiko. You are a celebrity now, Hachi. I mean Hachiko."

From that day on, people from all over Japan came to see *Chuken* Hachiko, the famous dog who sat in Shibuya Station waiting for his master. Many people who had fallen on hard times drew strength from meeting him. "If Hachiko does not give up hope, we will not give up hope," they said to one another. Many people stroked Hachiko's fur, believing that touching him would bring them good fortune. Those who could gave the Station Master money so that the *Akita-ken* would not go hungry. Everyone who met Hachiko was moved by his loyalty and devotion.

Years passed, and the Station Master and Yasuo were as devoted to Hachiko as he was to his master. Now that they had extra money to care for him, they were able to buy Hachiko treats from the food vendors outside the train station. Yasuo wandered up and down in front of the food stalls, deciding what to buy. Would Hachiko like a bowl of *udon*? No, the noodles might be too slippery for him. What about a serving of *oden*? *Tofu*, eggs, fish, and vegetables cooked in broth tasted good to Yasuo, but he did not think the dog would like it. He stopped in front of the *yakitori* stand and ordered a skewer of grilled chicken.

Hachiko leaped up and wagged his tail when he saw what Yasuo had brought him.

"Wait a minute, Hachiko," Yasuo laughed, holding the food up out of the dog's reach. "Let me take the chicken off the skewer and put it into your bowl."

But Hachiko did not want to wait. He jumped up and knocked the skewer out of Yasuo's hand. Then he stretched out on the platform, held the stick between his two front paws, and pulled off the pieces of chicken by himself.

"How clever you are," Yasuo said. "I have never seen a dog do that."

Yasuo went downstairs to buy another serving of *yakitori,* and asked the vendor to follow him back to the train station. He called the Station Master over to watch Hachiko eat.

"Look how smart he is." Yasuo pointed at Hachiko pulling the chicken off the skewer.

"Yes, he is very bright," Mr. Yoshikawa agreed. "And he had an excellent teacher," the Station Master reminded Yasuo.

"He may have a skewer of *yakitori* whenever he wants one," the food vendor said. "You do not have to pay me for it. It is my pleasure." He watched Hachiko

eat for another minute, then bowed good-bye and returned to his stand.

Another day, when Yasuo was a teenager, he and some classmates got off the train at Shibuya Station. "Yasuo, come play baseball with us," one of the boys said.

"I cannot," Yasuo said. "I have a responsibility." He gestured toward Hachiko, sitting on the platform.

The Station Master was standing nearby. "Go with them," Mr. Yoshikawa said. "I will take care of Hachiko today."

"Come with us, Yasuo!" his friend called again. "We are going to the park."

Yasuo looked at his schoolmates. Then he looked at Hachiko. The dog's brown eyes were so full of hope and so full of sadness. How could he desert him?

"I will meet you there later," he told his friends. "After I feed Hachiko."

Yasuo and the Station Master walked over to the golden-brown *Akita*. Mr. Yoshikawa reached down to pat the dog's head.

"You are very good to him," he said to Yasuo. "Someday he will reward you."

Yasuo laughed. How could Hachiko reward him?

"You will see," said Mr. Yoshikawa. "I do not know how and I do not know when, but I know it will happen. I have a strong feeling about it here." He pointed to his stomach. "Hachiko is a very loyal dog. You have treated him well. And I would be surprised if such a good deed went unrewarded."

Time passed, and Yasuo continued to help the Station Master take care of Hachiko. They gave him fresh food and water every day. They cleaned and brushed his fur. And most important, they made sure that everyone who touched him treated him with kindness.

Mr. Yoshikawa and Yasuo used some of the money people had given them to build a shelter for Hachiko behind the train station. Sometimes he slept in it, and sometimes he did not. Sometimes he arrived at the train station wet from the rain, or with bits of snow clinging to his fur. One day he sat perfectly still as a small earthquake rattled Shibuya Station.

Day after day, month after month, year after year, Hachiko sat on the platform, waiting. It seemed that nothing would ever stop him from meeting the three o'clock train.

One spring day, a few weeks after the cherry blossoms had bloomed, Yasuo arrived at the train station a little before three o'clock. He was sixteen years old now and he wore a handsome navy-blue uniform and a cap bearing his school's emblem over the brim. As soon as he stepped off the train, he went to see the Station Master.

"Come to my office, Yasuo, and I will get you some food for Hachiko." The Station Master moved slowly now, and his hair was as white as the rice he scooped into Hachiko's bowl. "Today is a very special day. Do you know why?"

Yasuo thought for a minute. It was the fifth day of the fifth month.

"It is *Tango-no-Sekku*," he said to the Station Master.

"Yes, it is Boys' Day," Mr. Yoshikawa said. "But there is another reason why today is special."

Yasuo thought again. "Is it your birthday?" he asked.

"No."

"Is it Hachiko's birthday?"

"No, but it does have something to do with Hachiko. Today marks exactly ten years that Hachiko has waited for the Professor."

"Ten years!" Yasuo shook his head. "There has never been a dog as loyal as Hachiko," he said to the Station Master.

Yasuo took Hachiko's bowl of food and walked over to the platform. Hachiko was lying on his side with his head resting on the ground. He was an old dog now, and the golden-brown fur around his muzzle had turned white. His left ear had begun to droop several years ago and was now almost bent in half. Hachiko had grown thin and was no longer able to sit up tall and straight. Sometimes he was too tired to climb the steps to the train station, and the *yakitori* vendor and the Station Master had to help him do it. Often he would be lying on the platform when Yasuo arrived. Sometimes he was even asleep.

"Hello, Hachiko," Yasuo said in a gentle voice as he squatted down to pet the dog's side. He could feel Hachiko's ribs beneath his fur. "Wake up, little friend," Yasuo said. "Do you know it has been ten years that you have waited for the Professor?"

The *Akita* opened his eyes and stared at Yasuo, but he did not lift his head.

"Hello, little friend. What a good dog you are," Yasuo said softly. "What a fine dog you are. Hachiko, you are the best dog in all of Japan."

As he stroked the side of Hachiko's face with his fingertips, the dog's right ear tilted forward at the sound of an approaching train.

"Do you want to get up, Hachiko?" Yasuo asked.

Hachiko looked at Yasuo, and then with great effort he struggled to his feet. The train appeared around the bend of the tracks, pulled up to the platform, and ground to a loud stop. Hachiko looked at it, sat up as tall and straight as he could, and opened his mouth.

"Wan-wan!" Hachiko barked loudly. *"Wan-wan!"* Then, all his strength gone, he sighed a great sigh and collapsed to the ground. ·

"Hachiko!" Yasuo cried as he watched the dog take a few shuddering breaths. His chest heaved up and down once, twice, three times . . . and then was still.

Yasuo ran to get the Station Master. "Hurry, we must help him!" he cried.

Mr. Yoshikawa came running. He knelt down by the dog and stroked Hachiko's great head. "It is too late," he said, his voice filled with sorrow.

A small crowd gathered around Hachiko's body. The *yakitori* vendor took off his *happi* jacket and handed it to Yasuo with a silent bow. Yasuo took the jacket and tenderly covered the dog with it. Then he turned his head and blinked his eyes rapidly. He was almost a grown man now, and he did not want to cry.

"Come with me," Mr. Yoshikawa said. He brought Yasuo into his office and had him sit down in a chair. The Station Master pulled up another chair for himself, and the two friends sat together side by side without speaking, each deep in thought.

After a while, the Station Master looked at Yasuo. "We feel sad for ourselves because we will not see Hachiko anymore," he said. "But there is a reason to feel happy too."

"What is there to feel happy about?" Yasuo asked, his eyes brimming with tears.

"Hachiko is no longer old, and he is no longer tired," answered Mr. Yoshikawa, who was a bit old and tired himself. "He has left his body, but his spirit is in a better place now."

"Do you really think so?" asked Yasuo.

"I will tell you what I think," the Station Master said, "though it is far from traditional, and it may even sound foolish." Mr. Yoshikawa paused and waited

while a train pulled into the station. "Do you hear that train?" he asked.

Yasuo nodded.

"I have been around trains all my life," Mr. Yoshikawa said, "and I have come to believe that there is a special train to bring those who have obtained Enlightenment up to Heaven. Every day for the past ten years, Professor Ueno has met this special train to see if his beloved *Akita-ken* is on it. Day after day after day he has waited up in Heaven, just as Hachiko has waited here on earth. And today, when the special train reaches Heaven and opens its doors, Hachiko will be the first one to step out. Just think how happy he will be to see his master again."

Yasuo smiled. "He will lick the Professor's fingers and then run in circles and make himself dizzy."

Mr. Yoshikawa smiled too and brushed away a tear. "I will miss him very much."

Yasuo nodded and wiped his wet cheeks. "So will I."

The day after Hachiko died, Yasuo came to the train station as he always did. He was so used to visiting Hachiko and the Station Master, he did not know what else to do. So he sat down on a wooden bench near the train tracks and looked at the passengers as they exited their trains. As he watched, two women dressed in flowered *kimonos* stepped onto the platform. They turned eagerly toward Hachiko's waiting place. When they saw that he was not there, they looked at each other in confusion. Yasuo rose from his bench and walked over to them.

"Hachiko's heart stopped beating yesterday," he said, bowing his head with grief.

"I am so sorry," both women said at once.

"The *Akita-ken* has died?" A student holding a stack of books in his arms stopped in his tracks, stunned.

"*Chuken* Hachiko is no longer with us," a young mother told her son.

Word of Hachiko's death spread quickly through Shibuya Station. As each train pulled up to the platform, the people who stepped off looked to Hachiko's spot as if they could not believe what they were being told. The expressions on their faces turned from hope to pain and sorrow as they saw that the news was true. It was almost more than Yasuo could bear.

Yasuo returned to the wooden bench and sat down wearily. He looked at Hachiko's spot and then shut his eyes. If only when he opened them he would see his little friend sitting up tall and straight among the crowd, his gaze fixed on the train tracks as he waited for his master. Yasuo squeezed his eyes shut even more tightly and then opened them again, hoping for a miracle. But Hachiko's spot was as empty as it had been just moments before.

Even though many people were getting off their trains, no one walked over the place where Hachiko had once waited. Yasuo slumped down on the bench, stared straight ahead, and watched person after person walk around Hachiko's spot, just as they had when he was alive. And then he got an idea.

He went to Mr. Yoshikawa's office and asked his friend to come sit with him on the wooden bench. "I have just thought of a way to bring Hachiko back," Yasuo said.

Mr. Yoshikawa looked at him, his eyebrows knitted together in puzzlement. "How?" he asked.

"Do you see the people getting off their trains?" asked Yasuo.

The Station Master nodded.

"Do you see how everyone looks at the spot where Hachiko used to sit?"

The Station Master nodded again.

"What if we built a statue of Hachiko and placed it on his spot?" Yasuo asked. "Then he will always be with us."

"That is a wonderful idea," said Mr. Yoshikawa. "But where will we find the money to pay for it?"

"Excuse me. I do not mean to intrude," said a man wearing thick black-framed glasses, "but I could not help overhearing your conversation. I do not have much money, but I miss seeing Hachiko sitting there. I will give you what I can to help build the statue." And with that, the man pressed a small silver coin with a hole in the middle worth five *sen* into the Station Master's white-gloved hand.

"I will give something too," a woman said, opening her pocketbook.

More and more people donated money, and again a story about Hachiko was printed in the newspaper. People from all over Japan were so moved by the tale of the loyal, faithful dog that they sent as much money as they could. After more newspaper stories were written, more people heard about Hachiko. People from as near as the next street over and as far away as the United States all sent money to help pay for a statue to be placed at Shibuya Station.

By the time the summer rains had ended, enough money had been collected to pay for the statue. After much discussion, a well-respected sculptor was selected for the job. He came to the train station to speak with Yasuo.

"Tell me about Hachiko," said the artist. "I understand you knew him best."

"This is where he waited," Yasuo said, showing the man the place where Hachiko used to sit. "And when he sat up, the top of his head came to about here." He put the flat of his hand up to his hip. "His eyes were deep-set and small, and his ears were shaped like triangles."

"Yes, I have seen the pictures in the newspapers," said the artist. "Can you tell me something about him I could not see in a photograph?"

Yasuo thought for a moment. "Hachiko was completely devoted to Professor Ueno," he said. "Many people wanted to adopt him, but he would not give his heart to anyone but his master."

"Ah, that is very helpful," said the sculptor, nodding.

"He was kind to all and treated everyone in the same manner," Yasuo went on. "It did not matter if you were a child or an adult. It did not matter if you were a man or a woman. It did not matter if you were rich or poor. If you wanted to touch Hachiko's fur for luck, he would allow it. He was gentle with everyone. He got upset only when someone tried to move him from his waiting spot."

"I see," said the artist. "Is there anything else?"

Yasuo shut his eyes, and a picture of Hachiko arose in his mind. "He was always very dignified," he said, swallowing hard. "Even at the end, when he could not sit up tall and straight. He always did his best."

"*Arigato*, Yasuo," the man said. "I now have what I need." And with a bow of thanks, he left the station.

The sculptor went to his studio at once. Day after day after day he locked himself inside his work space, but he would not permit anyone to enter.

"I will let you know when the sculpture is finished," he said whenever anyone came to his door.

Month after month went by, and still there was no word from the sculptor. Almost a whole year had passed since the day Hachiko had died, and it was spring again.

Then right after the cherry blossoms bloomed and fell from the trees, the artist announced that the statue was ready. It was covered with a white cloth and brought to Shibuya Station, where a great ceremony was held.

Trains scheduled to enter the station were halted between three and four o'clock. People started arriving at two-thirty, and by the time Yasuo and his parents reached the station an enormous crowd had gathered. People spilled over from the platform into the train station, down the steps, and onto the street.

Yasuo struggled to move through the solid wall of people like a carp swimming upstream. He looked back over his shoulder several times to make sure his mother and father were following him. At last they reached the platform and made their way over to the Station Master, who was standing next to Hachiko's waiting spot.

"There are so many people here," Yasuo said in amazement.

"Yes," said Mr. Yoshikawa. "There are teachers and students from Tokyo Imperial University who knew Professor Ueno. There are commuters who knew *Chuken* Hachiko." He pointed to a group of men holding their notebooks and cameras. "And there are also reporters."

At precisely three o'clock, a Shinto priest began the ceremony by saying a prayer that expressed gratitude for the ancestors. Then he asked that those gathered before him would be blessed with health, happiness, prosperity, and protection.

Next a man who had taught at the University alongside Professor Ueno said a few words.

"Professor Eizaburo Ueno loved the earth, and he loved all the plants, trees, and flowers that grow upon it," said the Professor's colleague. "He loved to teach, and he loved his students. But most of all, he loved his golden-brown *Akita-ken*."

The artist who had created the sculpture was next to address the crowd.

"Many of you have been curious about what I have been doing for the past year," he said. "You wondered why no noise came from my studio and why no supplies were carried in or out. This is because I had to prepare myself for the great task I was given." He gestured toward the statue, still hidden from view under its cloth. "I needed to sit still for many, many hours, just as Hachiko sat, in order to understand him and appreciate him," the artist said. "Only after I had experienced enough stillness and solitude did I feel ready to begin. And then I knew at once exactly what to do."

Finally Mr. Yoshikawa spoke. First, he thanked everyone who had donated money to build Hachiko's statue. "Without each and every one of you, this would not be possible," he said, spreading his arms wide. Then he motioned for Yasuo to join him. "I would like to present Yasuo Takahashi," the Station Master said to the people standing on the platform. "He was a great friend to Hachiko, and I am sure he has something to say."

Yasuo stood still and looked at the Station Master. Mr. Yoshikawa nodded, and motioned again.

"They are waiting, Yasuo," Mr. Takahashi whispered to his son.

"Just say what is in your heart," Mrs. Takahashi added.

Yasuo took a deep breath, stepped in front of the statue, and bowed his respects to the crowd.

"Hachiko taught us many things," he began, but then he had to stop. His voice was thick with tears, and his words sounded broken and shaky. Yasuo blinked his eyes and swallowed hard. The train station, usually such a noisy place, was completely quiet as Yasuo struggled to calm himself.

He looked into the crowd and noticed a little boy in a navy-blue sailor suit, holding his mother's hand. The boy looked to be about five years old, the same age Yasuo was on the day he first met the Professor and Hachiko. When the little boy saw Yasuo looking at him, his face broke into a smile. Yasuo smiled back and felt brave enough to go on.

"Hachiko taught us that we must never give up,"

Yasuo said. "He taught us about loyalty and devotion. He taught us about hope and faith. He taught us about patience and responsibility. But above all, Hachiko taught us the true meaning of friendship. It is for these reasons we honor him today."

Yasuo moved closer to the statue and asked Mr. Yoshikawa to join him. Together they removed the cloth and stepped back. Everyone gasped. The *Akita-ken* made of bronze raised high on a pedestal was Hachiko, sitting up tall and straight, his right ear thrust forward, his left ear drooping down, his eyes staring ahead.

Yasuo reached up to stroke the sculpture, half-expecting to feel soft fur instead of hard metal beneath his fingertips. "What a good dog you are," Yasuo whispered to the statue. "What a fine dog you are. Hachiko, you are the best dog in all of Japan."

New Year's Day, 1939
(Four Years Later)

To celebrate the New Year, the entrance to Shibuya Station was decorated with pine-tree branches to symbolize strength and bamboo to symbolize virtue. Yasuo, now a twenty-year-old student at Tokyo Imperial University, climbed the stairs to the station, carrying a gift of sweet *mochi* cakes wrapped in a blue *furoshiki* to give to Mr. Yoshikawa for the holiday.

There was a long line of travelers waiting to see the Station Master. Yasuo stepped out onto the platform and sat down on the wooden bench across from Hachiko's statue to wait for his friend. Where Yasuo sat was now known as the "Hachiko side" of the train station. It was not uncommon to hear one person say to another, "I will see you at Hachiko's statue after work," or "Meet me at Hachiko at six o'clock."

As Yasuo looked toward Hachiko's statue, he noticed a girl about his own age. She was tall, slender, and very pretty, and her cheeks were bright with cold. Her hair was fastened with an ornament of white paper flowers, and she wore an elegant silk *kimono* embroidered with delicate plum blossoms.

The girl stood with her back to Hachiko, glancing to her right and to her left. She looked up at the big clock hanging from the ceiling inside the train station and tapped her foot. Yasuo kept his eye on the girl as she waited. He knew it was rude to stare, but he could not turn away. The girl was scowling now, her forehead furrowed and her lips pointing down. Yasuo scowled as well.

As Yasuo gazed at her, the girl looked at the clock one last time, thrust her hands on her hips, and walked away. Before he knew what he was doing, he jumped to his feet.

"Wait!" he cried. The girl turned around and smiled. Yasuo noticed she had a dimple in her left cheek. It disappeared quickly when the girl saw a stranger had called to her. She turned on her heels and started out of the station.

"Wait!" Yasuo called again. "I know I am not the one you are waiting for," he said as he caught up to her. "But I would be honored if you would take a walk with me." He lowered his eyes and bowed. "My name is Yasuo Takahashi. Come, ask the Station Master. He will tell you I am respectable." He led her inside the station over to Mr. Yoshikawa's office.

"Happy New Year," Yasuo said, bowing to his friend. He gave Mr. Yoshikawa the gift he had brought. "I would like you to meet . . ."

"My name is Miyuki," the girl said with a bow to the Station Master.

"I am pleased to meet you," Mr. Yoshikawa said, returning the bow. "And I am pleased to see you have met my friend Yasuo. He is a fine young man: patient and devoted, loyal and responsible, known far and wide for his kindness." Mr. Yoshikawa smiled broadly. "And he is about to be rewarded for a very kind thing he did many years ago." The Station Master winked at Yasuo. "Make sure you tell Miyuki all about your friend Hachiko."

"The faithful dog?" Miyuki asked. "Did you know him?"

"Yes, I did," said Yasuo, leading Miyuki out of the station. As they walked, he told her all about Hachiko. And even though the day was windy and cold, they walked and talked all afternoon.

Yasuo and Miyuki spent the next afternoon together, and the afternoon after that as well. Soon they were spending all their time together. Soon they fell in love.

Yasuo and Miyuki were together in the spring, when the cherry blossoms bloomed, and in the summer, when the rains came. They were together in the fall, when the leaves changed color, and in the winter, when the snow fell. Yasuo brought Miyuki home to meet his family. His mother and father thought she was a fine young woman. Miyuki brought Yasuo home to meet her family. Her mother and father thought he was a fine young man.

A year passed, and Yasuo asked Miyuki to meet him at Hachiko's statue in Shibuya Station on New Year's Day at three o'clock. He said he had something very important to ask her.

Yasuo arrived at the statue at five minutes to three. He stood beside Hachiko, looking to his right, to his left, and to his right again, searching the steady stream of travelers for the one face that would make his belly tremble with joy. At last he saw Miyuki coming toward him, and the sight of her made his own face light up like the sun.

"Hello, Miyuki," Yasuo said. He took both her hands in his and stared into her lovely dark eyes.

"Hello, Yasuo," Miyuki said. "What is it you have to ask me?"

Yasuo cleared his throat several times before he spoke. "Miyuki," he said. "Soon I will finish my studies, and then"—Yasuo squeezed her hands tightly—"and then . . . will you marry me? I promise that if you say yes, I will be as devoted to you as Hachiko was to Professor Ueno for all the days of my life."

Yasuo and Miyuki both turned toward the statue of Hachiko sitting up so tall and proud. Then they turned back toward each other.

Miyuki looked into Yasuo's eyes. Her lips curved up into a smile, and the dimple he loved so well appeared in her left cheek. "Yes, Yasuo, I will marry you," she said, her voice full of happiness. "And I promise that for all the days of my life, I will be as devoted to you as you were to *Chuken* Hachiko, the faithful dog of Japan."

AUTHOR'S NOTE

Hachiko Waits is a work of fiction inspired by a true story.

In January 1924, Professor Eizaburo Ueno adopted a three-month-old *Akita* puppy and named him Hachi. The Professor traveled to work by train, and every day Hachi accompanied him to the train station. After the Professor's train left, Hachi ran home. And every day he returned to Shibuya Station just before three o'clock to meet his master.

One day in May of 1925, Professor Ueno died unexpectedly at work. Hachi waited at the train station for his master to come home that day and every day after that for approximately ten years. Although Yasuo and his family are fictional characters, many people, including Mr. Yoshikawa, cared for Hachiko, as he came to be called, over the next decade. He died of natural causes while waiting for his master.

The people of Japan were so impressed by Hachiko's loyalty that they decided to erect a statue in his honor and to place it at Shibuya Station. Money was raised and an artist named Teru Ando was hired. In 1934, just about a year before Hachiko died, a ceremony attended by many people was held to dedicate the statue.

During World War II, Hachiko's statue was melted down so that the metal could be used in the war effort. After the war, Takeshi Ando, the sculptor Teru Ando's son, created a new, identical statue to replace the original one, and another dedication ceremony attended by an enormous crowd was held.

This second statue is still at Shibuya Station, and it is a very popular meeting place. Over the years it has become a tradition for young couples to pledge their loyalty to each other in front of Hachiko's statue.

Though many years have passed since Hachiko waited for Professor Ueno at the train station, he has not been forgotten. To this day, his story is taught to schoolchildren all over Japan. And every year on April 8, a memorial service is held at Shibuya Station to honor *Chuken* Hachiko, the faithful dog of Japan.

GLOSSARY

When pronouncing Japanese words, the consonants sound just as they do in English. (The letter *g* is always said as in the word "gift," never as in "gentle.") The vowels are pronounced as follows:

> *a* is pronounced *ah* as in "far";
> *e* is pronounced *eh* as in "pet";
> *i* is pronounced *ee* as in "meet";
> *o* is pronounced *oh* as in "ocean";
> *u* is pronounced *oo* as in "moon."

In the words *Okaasan* and *Otoosan* the repeated vowels are called long vowels. They are pronounced as above (*ah* and *oh*) with the sound held twice as long as regular vowels, which are short and clipped. This is indicated below by a bar over the vowel.

Akita (*ah-kee-tah*). A breed of dog with erect ears and curled tail, native to Akita Prefecture, a region of northern Japan.
Akita-ken (*ah-kee-tah-kehn*). Akita dog.
Arigato (*ah-ree-gah-toh*). Thank you.
Chuken (*choo-kehn*). Faithful dog.
Furoshiki (*foo-roh-shee-kee*). Cloth bundle tied in a knot that can be used to hold one's possessions or to wrap a gift.
Futon (*foo-tohn*). Sleeping pad made of cotton or silk.
Genkan (*gehn-kahn*). Entrance hall.

Geta (*geh-tah*). Clogs made of plain wood with a V-shaped thong between the big toe and the remaining toes.

Hachi (*hah-chee*). Eight; also the original name of Professor Ueno's dog.

Happi (*hah-pee*). A short jacket, chiefly worn by workmen.

Honshu (*hohn-shoo*). Largest of the four islands that make up Japan.

Ichi, ni, san, shi, go (*ee-chee, nee, sahn, shee, goh*). One, two, three, four, five.

Kanji (*kahn-jee*). Chinese characters, based on pictures, used in Japanese writing.

Keyaki (*keh-yah-kee*). A tree native to Japan that grows very straight and tall, with yellow blossoms (known in the United States as a Japanese zelkova tree).

Kimono (*kee-moh-noh*). A full-length, robelike traditional Japanese garment with wide sleeves, fastened at the waist with a sash called an *obi*, worn by men, women, and children.

Miso (*mee-soh*). A paste made from beans and fermented rice, used to make soup.

Miyuki (*mee-yoo-kee*). A female name with several meanings: "deep snow," "calm silence," "tranquillity," and "beauty."

Mochi (*moh-chee*). Rice cake.

Obi (*oh-bee*). Wide, decorative sash worn around the waist over one's *kimono*.

Oden (*oh-dehn*). Boiled tofu, eggs, fish, and vegetables cooked for a long time in broth.

Okaasan (*oh-kāh-sahn*). Mother.

Otoosan (*oh-tōh-sahn*). Father.

Sen (*sehn*). A small denomination of Japanese money, similar to a penny.

Shibuya (*shee-boo-yah*). A district of Tokyo.

Shinto (*sheen-toh*). A religion practiced widely in Japan that stresses worship of nature and the spirits of ancestors (literally means "the way of the gods").

Tango-no-Sekku (*tahn-goh-noh-seh-koo*). Boys' Day (now celebrated as Children's Day).

Tatami (*tah-tah-mee*). Woven straw mats used to cover the wooden floor of a room.

Tempura (*tehm-poo-rah*). Seafood and vegetables dipped in batter and deep-fried.

Tofu (*toh-foo*). Soybean curd.

Udon (*oo-dohn*). Wheat noodles.

Wan-wan (*wahn-wahn*). Woof-woof; the sound of a dog's bark.

Yakitori (*yah-kee-toh-ree*). Bite-sized pieces of marinated chicken that are grilled on skewers.

Yasuo (*yah-soo-oh*). A male name meaning "tranquillity."

Zori (*zoh-ree*). Sandals made of straw with a V-shaped thong between the big toes and the remaining toes.

ACKNOWLEDGMENTS

For going above and beyond the call of duty cheerfully and with great enthusiasm, I offer an enormous *arigato* to Elise Feeley of the reference department at Forbes Library in Northampton, Massachusetts, who has never once in twenty years failed to find the answer to a research question; Joanne Yoshida, who also answered many questions and provided innumerable valuable insights; and Yasuko Fukumi, who so kindly invited me into her home and so generously shared her time, knowledge, and intelligence with me.

I am also grateful to my awesome agent, Elizabeth Harding; my extraordinary editor, Nina Ignatowicz, and her able assistant, Robin Tordini; and the wise and wonderful women in my writing group: Ann Turner, Anna Kirwan, Barbara Diamond Goldin, Corinne Demas, Jane Yolen, and Patricia MacLachlan, all of whom have blessed me with numerous gifts of kindness.

To the enormously talented Machiyo Kodaira, whose lovely illustrations add so much to *Hachiko Waits*, I bow my head in gratitude.

A very special thank-you goes to Polly Severance of Northfield, Massachusetts, who allowed me to be photographed with her beautiful champion *Akita*, Kumatama's Aojiroi Nikko, "Nico," whose name when translated from the Japanese means "pale sunlight."

And finally, as always, I give heartfelt thanks to Tzivia Gover for her listening ear and Mary Vazquez for her amazing grace.